TO: Henry
It was a pleasure meeting you.
I hope that the book encourages
you to clean your space. Thank
you for your support. Have a wonderful
day.

2021

The Mess

Written by Alicia Smith
Illustrated by Olivia Smith H.

Marie and Elise were chasing each other outside, and they began to hear a noise coming from the tree. They ran toward the tree and they saw birds chirping in a nest.

Elise and Marie stopped, then looked up the tree. Elise thought the birds were crying for their mom and feeling scared. Marie thought the birds were hungry and wanted food.

Ms. Kangaroo calls for Marie and Elise from the door, "Do you want to take a nature walk?" Marie and Elise shouted "Yes!", and they ran toward their mom with excitement.

While walking on the trail, Marie and Elise found rocks, sticks, leaves, and flowers. They also saw a rabbit that they tried to catch but it was too fast. Eventually, they got tired and wanted to go home.

Marie and Elise were thrilled to take their items home so they could do an art project. While sitting at the table, Marie and Elise colored pictures of their treasures that they found. Marie enjoyed drawing a Pink flower and Elise drew a blue bird.

Ms. Kangaroo said, "It's clean up time." Marie shouted out loud, "I don't want to clean up! Can I play in my room instead?" "If you want to play in your room, you must clean your mess" and Marie began cleaning.

Marie and Elise went to their room to play but minutes later, they ran out of the room shouting they could not find their teddy bears. They began to cry and hugged their mom's legs.

Ms. Kangaroo hugged Marie and Elise. "Let's walk to your room and look for the bears. Your room is a disaster! The bears must be hiding somewhere in your room. We will look for the bears together."

"Let's play the clean-up game! I will set a timer for 10 minutes and play music. We will see who finds their bear first before the timer goes off. Does that sound like a good idea"? Marie and Elise shouted, "Yes!"

Marie and Elise jumped up and down. Marie picked up toys and books. Elise picked up clothes and shoes. They began dancing together while cleaning their mess.

The timer went off and the mess was cleaned. Ms. Kangaroo gave Elise and Marie a huge hug. "You both were great helpers and showed good teamwork." Marie found her bear under a pile of clothes. Elise found her bear under a toy chest.

Ms. Kangaroo told Elise and Marie that it was time for bed. "We had a busy and fun day. Can you find a book that you both can agree on so we can have our nighttime story?" They found their favorite book to read and quietly listened to the story.

CPSIA information can be obtained
at www.ICGtesting.com
Printed in the USA
LVRC100234231021
701275LV00003B/32